Master Will

and the

Spanish Spy

Master Will and the Spanish Spy

TONY BRADMAN

Barrington  Stoke

First published in 2016 in Great Britain by
Barrington Stoke Ltd
18 Walker Street, Edinburgh, EH3 7LP

www.barringtonstoke.co.uk

Text © 2016 Tony Bradman
Illustration © 2016 Tom Morgan-Jones

A CIP catalogue record for this book is available
from the British Library upon request

ISBN: 978-1-78112-567-0

Printed in China by Leo

CONTENTS

"I see riot and dishonour stain the brow
Of my young Harry ..."

(Henry IV Part 1)

Chapter 1
Enter the Players

Stratford-upon-Avon, 1578

Will was the first boy in the class to hear the music.

He twisted round to see if anyone else had heard it too. It was a warm day in June and the classroom windows were wide open, but the other boys were day-dreaming or dozing.

Will could make out the beating of drums, the whistling of pipes and the tooting of trumpets coming from the bridge over the River Avon, the main road into the town. He

could hear somebody shouting, but the words weren't clear. All of a sudden Will realised what was happening and a thrill ran down his spine. Then the other boys heard the music too, and everyone perked up.

They'd been at their desks since six o'clock that morning with Doctor Pinch the schoolmaster droning on at them. He stood before them in his long black gown, looking like a bat – a short, plump, boring bat. He was reading a poem about a Greek hero in the underworld, but Will couldn't keep his mind on the story, no matter how hard he tried.

At last even Doctor Pinch noticed the beat of the drums. He slammed down his book and scowled at the boys. They ignored him and the buzz of whispering in the classroom grew louder.

"Silence!" the teacher yelled. He grabbed a cane and the nearest boys ducked as it swished over their heads. They were used to it – mean old Pinch hit someone almost every day.

Doctor Pinch opened his mouth to yell again but the ringing of the school bell drowned him out. The boys stampeded for the door like a herd of bulls, with Will in the lead.

Will dashed down the stairs two at a time, out the school gate and into the street, with his schoolmates pelting along behind him. The drums and whistles and pipes grew louder still. The streets were filling up with people – young and old, rich and poor – as everyone rushed towards the market square.

It wasn't a market day, so the square was empty of stalls. There were three big wagons pulled by teams of horses on one side, and a crowd was gathering on the other, in front of

the Guildhall. The town council met there, and Will's father did business there too. Although, if truth be told, he did more business in the Boar's Head tavern next door.

Will pushed his way to the front of the crowd and saw a dozen men and boys in the middle of the square. Some were playing instruments, others were tumbling or dancing, and all were dressed in bright, colourful clothes. Will's heart surged with joy – *the travelling players had arrived!*

For every summer that Will could remember, companies of players had come to Stratford. They would stay a few days, then move on. Will's mother would always give him a penny so he could watch them sing and dance, do acrobatic displays and play the fool. But he liked it best when they acted out stories. They transformed themselves with spark and fire into completely different people.

As the music stopped one of the men stepped forward. He wore a red jacket and a tall peacock feather gleamed on one side of his hat. He had a dark beard flecked with grey and his round belly and friendly smile gave him the look of a man who liked a flagon of beer and a good dinner. His deep voice boomed out around the square and the crowd fell silent and listened.

"We are the Earl of Leicester's men from London. I am James Burbage, Chief Player. We are here to bring joy to your lives, starting tonight with our first performance. Let me introduce you to the company ..."

The crowd around Will murmured. The Earl of Leicester was a very powerful nobleman, a favourite of Queen Elizabeth herself.

Each player stepped forward and took a bow as Burbage called his name. Some did

it with a flourish, or a little dance, or a tune on an instrument. Two were Burbage's sons, Cuthbert and Richard. Cuthbert was tall and dark and older than Will. Richard was shorter and fairer, and looked to be around Will's age. As Will watched, his eyes met Richard's.

"Tonight," Burbage said, "you'll find us at one of your finest taverns, the Swan Inn, at six o'clock." He picked out a man in the crowd. "Will you be coming, my friend? And you, sir? What about you, young lady?" Each person he spoke to grinned and nodded.

Then Burbage pointed at Will. "You there, what's your name, lad?"

"Er ... W-W-Will Shakespeare," Will stammered, and he felt himself blush.

"Never heard of you!" Burbage said, and the crowd laughed. "But what's in a name,

eh? If you're the first in the queue at the Swan tonight I'll let you in for free – and four others too!"

The crowd gave a great cheer.

"I'll be there!"

Chapter 2
The Old Ways

Will raced back home to Henley Street. As he approached the house, the stink of tanning leather from his father's glove-making business hit him.

John Shakespeare also lent money, dealt in wool, and a lot more besides. Mary Shakespeare ran the home, and looked after Will and his four younger brothers and sisters – Gilbert, Joan, Anne and Richard. As Will rushed in the door, she handed him a bowl of broth. Will patted her head – now he was tall enough to do it, it had become a joke between them.

"No need to ask where you've been," she said. "I heard the music."

Will told her about the players from London as he ate.

"Is Father at home?" he said. "I'd like to tell him about the players too."

"He is, but he's in a foul temper," Will's mother said. "A letter came for him this morning and he's done nothing but stew since it arrived."

Will was used to his father's moods – they all were. John Shakespeare could be as happy as a lark one minute, and like a grumpy bear the next. Will smiled, but his mother didn't smile back. He saw the worry cloud her eyes.

But of course she worried about lots of things – lazy servants, her hens not laying, rats in the thatch. Like all mothers, she worried

every time one of her children got a cough or a fever. But this worry seemed different. It was darker and deeper.

"Who was the letter from?" Will said. "Did Father say what it was about?"

"No, he didn't. But I pray it doesn't mean trouble ..."

As she spoke, she made the Sign of the Cross. Will wished she wouldn't. If the servants saw her, they'd know she was a Catholic, and that was against the law now in England. People were so suspicious of Catholic countries, enemies of England like Spain, and they thought there were Catholic spies hiding everywhere. In Queen Elizabeth's England, it didn't pay to stand out from the crowd, as far as religion was concerned.

Will's father was in his office, sitting at his battered and cluttered oak desk. Will stood in the doorway looking at him as he frowned down at a letter.

"Father?" he said. "I've come to give you some good news."

His father looked up and smiled. "I'm glad to hear it, Will," he said. "I couldn't cope if this day got any worse."

"You'll soon cheer up when you hear what I've got to tell you –" Will began.

His father broke in. "Those toads at the College of Heralds have turned down our request for a Coat of Arms again! I've a good mind to take them to court. I've as much right to a Coat of Arms as anybody ..."

He raged on, but Will had heard it all before. A Coat of Arms told the world that your

family was a force to be reckoned with. John Shakespeare was desperate for one, but he was convinced that the College of Heralds were a bunch of snobs who looked down their noses at him because he had been born poor.

"A company of players has arrived from London," Will said when his father had stopped at last. "They'll be at the Swan tonight. Father, can we all go?"

"No," his father said. "Nobody from this family will watch any players at a common inn, is that clear?"

Will scowled back at him – and then the argument began.

Chapter 3
The Very Idea of Fun

"I don't understand," Will said. "We saw the players last year."

"Well, that's where I've been going wrong," his father said. "Only the most respectable families are granted a Coat of Arms – and respectable families don't go to see travelling players. They're no better than thieves and beggars."

"But, Father, all the town will be there tonight," Will said. "Rich and poor."

"Maybe so, but I don't think Sir Thomas Lucy will be there with his family, do you?" Will's father said. He leaned back in his chair, convinced he'd won the argument.

Will knew he was right. Sir Thomas Lucy ran the Council, and he wouldn't be seen dead at a performance by travelling players. He hated the very idea of anybody having fun.

"Good," Will said. "The less I see of his sour old face the better."

"Why, you cheeky whippersnapper," his father roared. "How dare you ..."

The shouting went on until Will's mother appeared at the door. "Calm down before you have a fit, John," she said. "Edmund is here."

"Edmund?" Will's father said. He picked up some papers from his desk with a shifty look on his face. "Er ... did he say what he wanted?"

"No." Will's mother stared at her husband with narrowed eyes. "Get back to school, Will."

Will took the hint. He had no desire to be in the house while his Uncle Edmund was around. He was a nasty, grasping man. He was sitting stiffly at the kitchen table as Will went out the door, and barely nodded a greeting at his nephew.

Will was still brooding when the school bell rang at five o'clock. He trudged home, pushing past the excited crowds heading to the Swan Inn. Will was torn between his duty to his father and his desire to see the players.

Will turned round and ran, worried he'd left it too late. He took shortcuts down alleys, climbed over walls, dashed through gardens, hurdled the tombstones behind Holy Trinity

Church. He ran so fast that he was at the
gates to the Swan with half an hour to spare.
He claimed his place as first in the queue and
stood there panting. James Burbage strode out
and smiled at him.

"Young Master Shakespeare, isn't it?
Good to see you!" he said. Will felt a surge
of pleasure that Burbage had remembered
his name. "Step right in, free of charge as
promised!"

Will ran in and found a place right in front
of the stage. A woodland scene hung from the
balcony behind the stage.

The courtyard came alive with talk and
laughter, shouts and gossip. At last, the crowd
settled down and Burbage's son Richard strode
onto the stage. He gazed out and spoke.

"In Sherwood Forest lies our scene,
The home of outlaws dressed in green.
An evil Sheriff drives our tale.
Will he succeed or will he fail?
The villain's bitter hate and rage
Will be the traffic of our stage.
So come with us into the wood,
And there you'll meet ... good ROBIN HOOD!"

Chapter 4
A Midsummer's Night

That night Will stood there at the edge of the stage, totally rapt. He had never experienced anything like *The True Tale of Robin Hood and his Merry Men*. He had forgotten that he was watching players. They made the crowd laugh with delight and shiver with fear as they brought the story they all knew so well to life.

Burbage's son Cuthbert was Robin Hood, an excellent hero with a wicked sense of humour. Richard was a truly convincing Maid Marian – in this play, as in all others, female roles were played by boys. Burbage himself was a dark

and evil villain. The crowd booed and hissed at him each time he strode on stage. One other player was rather wooden and clumsy, but he only had a minor part.

All too soon, Robin Hood defeated the Sheriff and married Maid Marian. Then the whole company came on stage to dance a wild jig that had the crowd clapping and cheering and whistling.

At last the courtyard was empty. The sky above the inn was dark and Will knew he should head for home before he got into real trouble.

"Well then, Master Shakespeare," a voice said. "Did you enjoy the show?"

Will turned and saw Burbage still in his Sheriff costume, but with a mug of ale in his hand now.

"Yes," Will said, smiling. "It was the best play I've ever seen."

"I'm very glad to hear it," Burbage said, and he raised his mug to Will. "I hope you'll tell everybody about us. Now, how would you like to meet the lads?"

Will was so thrilled that he didn't trust himself to speak. He nodded and followed Burbage as he strode off into the inn. The inn was packed with townsfolk drinking and laughing and talking. They grinned at Burbage and slapped him on the back as he went past.

The rest of the players were in the far corner of the inn. "Budge up there, Richard," said Burbage, nudging his younger son. "I've found you a friend."

"You've certainly found *something*, Father," Richard said, and he looked Will up and down.

"You two will get along fine – I can feel it in my bones," said Burbage. "Ho there!" he called out to the landlord. "A jug of ale if you will!"

Richard shuffled along the bench so Will could sit down, and a serving boy plonked a plate of meat and a foaming mug of ale in front of him. He took a sip. The ale was much stronger than the small beer his family drank at home.

Some of the talk round the table was the usual banter of men and boys. But Will found their talk about the play fascinating. He was surprised to hear that one of the players had forgotten his words, and that another had come onstage at the wrong moment.

"I see you're taking all this in, young Master Shakespeare," Burbage said. "First in the crowd to greet us, first in the queue to get in, and now

hanging around afterwards. I wonder if you might have ambitions to be a player yourself?"

Will stared at him. The idea thrilled him. It was as if a door had swung open in his mind, letting him glimpse a different future. Then he remembered his father's words. *They're no better than thieves and beggars.*

"I wish I could," he said. "But my father wouldn't stand for it."

"Is that so?" Burbage said with a grin. "Don't tell me – your father wants you to be a proper gentleman and go to university. I'm sure he looks down on us players. I've heard all the insults. But we make folk happy, and that can't be a bad thing. You mark my words – there's more than one way to get on in life. And where do you think you're going, Francis Peele?"

Burbage turned away from Will to speak to a young man who had stood to leave the table. Will recognised him as the clumsy player. Up close, he had a lean and hungry look.

"I need a little air," Francis Peele muttered. "This inn feels rather stuffy."

Burbage shrugged and Peele walked off, and then Burbage turned back to Will. "Now then, Master Shakespeare," he said. "Isn't it time you went home?"

He was right and Will knew he couldn't put it off any longer.

All the way home he tried to think of how to save himself when he got there. He almost bumped into Francis Peele, who was standing in a doorway talking to an older man. As Will walked past, something caught his eye. Francis Peele was holding a string of black beads with a

silver cross hanging from it. It was something Will's mother had too, but she kept it hidden deep in her skirt pockets. A rosary. Banned by law and punishable by death.

Chapter 5
Sun and Moon

Will stopped and stared at the two men. The older man looked up, then yanked Peele into the house.

Will shook himself and kept on walking. He told himself that what he'd seen meant nothing. So what if Francis Peele was a Catholic? For all Will knew, Burbage and the rest of the players might be Catholics too. So long as they kept it to themselves no harm would be done.

But the encounter left Will feeling unsettled. He knew Peele wasn't from Stratford – if he was, he would have heard of

him. But the older man *was* from the town –
Will had seen him around. So what was the
link between the two men? And why had Peele
been clutching that rosary?

Will thought, too, of the strange way
Burbage had treated Peele in the Swan. It had
been as clear as day that Burbage didn't like
him.

At home, Will opened the back door, took
a deep breath and peered into the kitchen. It
was empty, so he slipped inside and shut the
door. He tiptoed into the house, fully expecting
to be yelled at.

He heard muffled voices coming from
another room. Will crept up to the door and
put his ear against it to listen. His mother was
shouting and his father was grumbling back at
her.

"They've been arguing for hours," Will's brother Gilbert said. "We can't sleep."

Will looked round and saw his brothers and sisters on the stairs in their night-clothes. Joan and Anne and Richard were wide-eyed and snivelling, their pale cheeks wet with tears. Will hated to see them in such a state.

"Please make them stop, Will," Anne said. Will loved all his brothers and sisters, but he had a special place in his heart for little Anne.

"Come on, you lot," he said, and he shooed them back up the stairs. "You should be in bed. There's nothing to worry about ..."

Will settled the younger three back in their beds, blew out their candles and went to the room he shared with Gilbert.

"Did Mother and Father notice I wasn't here earlier?" he asked his brother.

"I don't know," Gilbert said. "They've been too busy yelling at each other. I've never known Mother so burned up with rage at Father."

Long after Gilbert was asleep, Will lay awake and wondered what had made his mother so angry. Usually his parents' bickering was like a summer storm, over almost before it had begun. This had sounded a lot more serious.

Will had a restless night of strange dreams. He woke with a thick head, and crept downstairs to the kitchen. He half expected his parents to be arguing again, or for them to ask where he'd been the night before. His mother was watching the maid serve breakfast to his brothers and sisters. The children were quiet, and Will's mother looked very pale.

"Good morning, Mother," Will said as he sat at the table. "Where's Father?"

"How should I know?" she said, with a frown. "Your father does as he pleases. But I do know where *you* were last night. You went to see the players, didn't you?"

"I did," Will murmured, his cheeks burning. "I'm sorry, I know Father said ..."

"I don't care what your father said," his mother snapped. "You can see them whenever you want!"

Will knew he should have been pleased, but his mother's cross tone made him feel very uneasy. She never took his side against his father. She never encouraged him to disobey him. Of course he wanted to see the players again, but he hated the idea that his parents

were so deep in conflict. It felt wrong, as if the sun and moon were at loggerheads.

At school the classroom buzzed with talk of the players. But Doctor Pinch seemed determined to bore his class to death with Latin grammar. Will soon decided he wouldn't go back to school after the midday break. He'd go to the Swan to see what the players were up to instead.

The players were in the courtyard of the inn when Will arrived. Several were on the stage reading aloud from rolls of parchment. Burbage was making comments from time to time. Will felt Francis Peele's eyes on him, but the young player turned away when Will met his gaze.

"Ah, if it isn't young Master Shakespeare again!" Burbage laughed, slapping him on the back. "You just can't stay away, can you? As

you're so keen you'd better make yourself useful. Richard, you're in charge of our latest recruit."

"Why thank you, Father," Richard said, and he bowed. "Come with me, recruit."

Half an hour later, Will was sitting in one of the company's wagons, helping Richard sort their old costumes. They were to check them for wear and tear and decide which ones could be repaired. Will realised he was being tested. Richard made sure the costumes he gave Will to check were the sweatiest and smelliest. As he worked, it was clear to Will what tricks the players performed to bring their plays to life – there was nothing rich about these costumes close up. They glittered but were not gold.

"Tell me," Will said after a while. "What were you doing when I arrived?"

"Oh, just trying out a new play," Richard said.

"How do you do that, then?" Will asked.

"It's simple," Richard said. "The place we always start is the story ..."

Will forgot all about the costumes as Richard explained how the company would decide on a story they'd like to turn into a play – a tale that was exciting or funny or well-known. Then someone wrote the story out in parts, the players learned the words and actions, and they practised and practised so it would all flow smoothly in a performance.

"What's it like?" Will said. "To be in a play, I mean."

"Why, it's the best feeling in the world," Richard said. "That's the short and long of it."

Will wasn't at all surprised to hear that. The more he thought about it, the more he wanted to experience that feeling for himself.

Chapter 6
A Dangerous Man

That same night, Will went to see the players perform again. This time the play was *Grandma Gurton's Needle*, a comedy full of daft characters and even dafter jokes, but Will found it just as magical as *Robin Hood*.

After the show, Will said a reluctant "no" when Burbage asked him to join the company for a drink and raced straight home instead. Whatever his mother said, his father would be angry if he found out where he'd been. But as luck would have it, his father was out – "on business" Will's mother said. Will sensed that things were still sour between his parents.

The next few days were rosy for Will. Burbage announced that the players would stay in Stratford for another week – "as we're so popular!" Will slipped away from school every afternoon, and spent as much time at the Swan as he could.

"Here, take this," Richard said one afternoon as they sat on the edge of the stage, and he handed Will a roll of parchment. "You can help me learn my lines. Hold on! You *can* read, can't you? I keep forgetting that I'm not in London any more ..."

"Yes, Richard, I can read." Will sighed. He was used to Richard's teasing talk of country bumpkins. "Probably better than you, in fact."

"Is that right?" Richard said with a smirk. "Well, we'll see about that."

Will smiled when he saw that the play was called *The Terrible Tragedy of Hector, Prince of*

Troy. He knew the story well, and he knew how to say all of the long Greek names. Richard was playing Helen of Troy, and Will read everyone else's part.

They both got so caught up in the drama that they acted out a fight scene for the joy of it. For a moment it felt as if Will really was in front of the mighty walls of Troy, fighting a deadly duel with his enemy.

"Your time has come, great Hector," Will read out, "and so you die ..."

Behind him somebody started clapping. Will turned and saw Burbage, with Cuthbert at his side. He felt himself blush.

"Well done, lad," Burbage said with a broad grin. "You spoke those lines like a true player."

"Then let's take him into the company instead of Richard," Cuthbert said.

"Very funny," Richard said, his eyes still on Will. "The boy is good, I'll give you that. But he's got a lot to learn, so you'll be stuck with me a while yet."

"And for my sins I'm stuck with the pair of you," Burbage said. "Now look lively – there's a mountain of work to do …"

Will left them to it, and headed home, whistling a merry tune to himself. Then the tune died on his lips. He had spotted Francis Peele – again. The young player always seemed to be whispering to people in shadowy corners, or peering about him as he slipped into a house.

Will had asked Richard about Peele, but all Richard could tell him was that Burbage had taken him on a month or two ago because they'd been short of players – three of their men had been struck down by the plague in

London. But no one liked him. He had an odd way about him, didn't rub along with the company and had turned out to be a poor player who stumbled over both his words and his actions.

Will remembered how Burbage had praised *him* – Will Shakespeare – as a "true player", and he struck up his merry whistle again. He forgot about Francis Peele.

For now.

Early the next day a visitor came to the Shakespeares' house. There was a pounding on the front door, and Will opened it to find a scrawny man outside. He had a wispy beard and all his clothes were black – his breeches, his jacket, his cloak and his tall hat with its

wide brim. He looked like a bad-tempered crow.

"Tell your father Sir Thomas Lucy wants to see him, boy," the man said. His voice was high and harsh. "Fetch the rest of your family too. I need to speak to you all."

Will's father jumped at the news that Sir Thomas was in the house, and he rushed to meet him. "Welcome to our humble home, Sir Thomas," he said. "What a great honour. Can I offer you something to eat or drink?"

"No," Sir Thomas snapped. "This isn't a social visit. I need to speak to you about an important matter, Shakespeare, and it would be best between the two of us." Will saw his mother look daggers at his father. "But first I want to give you and your family a warning."

Sir Thomas glowered round at them, as dramatic as any player. Then he went on.

"I have it from the best sources that a dangerous man might be in our district. Word has come from London that a Catholic priest – an Englishman, an exile who has returned in secret – is here in Stratford. This man could be a spy for the Spanish or an assassin sent to kill our good Queen."

Sir Thomas paused and fixed his eyes on Will's mother, who returned his stare. "There are people who would help such a ruthless villain," Sir Thomas hissed. "People who are still Catholics in their hearts. We must all be on the look-out for anyone suspicious. Is that understood?"

Everyone nodded.

"Excuse me, Sir Thomas," Will said. "What will happen to this dangerous man if he's caught?"

"He'll be hanged, drawn and quartered," Sir Thomas said. He was licking his lips with relish.

Will knew what being hanged, drawn and quartered meant. First they strung you up by the neck, then they pulled you down before you were dead. Next they ripped you open, yanked your guts out and burned them in front of your eyes. Finally they hacked your body into quarters, cut your head off and stuck it on a pike. It was a hideous death.

"Now as I said, Shakespeare," Sir Thomas went on, "a word ..."

Will's father led Sir Thomas off to his office.

Will barely saw them go.

His mind was full of Francis Peele again.

Chapter 7
This Rascal Boy

Will sat alone in his bedroom and brooded.
Was Francis Peele the dangerous man Sir
Thomas had been talking about? Could he be
a spy or even an assassin? He was certainly a
Catholic, and Will had seen him behaving oddly.
But Will had no real proof of anything more.
He would have to speak to his parents, even
if that meant he would have to confess to his
father that he had disobeyed him.

Will waited until he heard Sir Thomas leave
the house, and he went to find them.

They were in the kitchen, by the fire. Will stood in the shadows, listening.

"I hate that man," his mother was saying, her voice full of fear. "What did he want to talk to you about?"

"Nothing," Will's father said. "Well, it was *something*, just a bit of business, nothing to concern you ..."

"You told me it didn't concern me when you went to Edmund behind my back," Will's mother snapped. "I've never trusted him, and you shouldn't either."

Will didn't understand why his mother was so angry. After all, Uncle Edmund was family – and surely family helped each other.

"But this search for a Spanish spy ..." Will's mother went on. "Did you see the look in Sir

Thomas's eyes? He's always hated us. He's always known we helped Keating disappear."

"Hush, Mary," Will's father said. "We've always been careful. But you *must* avoid any contact with this secret priest. They *will* catch him, then they'll torture him to find out who he's talked to. Then those people will be tortured too, and killed ..."

Will slipped away, his mind in a whirl. If Francis Peele was a secret priest and a spy, then Burbage and Richard and Cuthbert and the rest of the company – and even Will – were in real danger. But he couldn't drag his parents into this mess too. There was only one person he could talk to.

Will found Burbage alone in a back room of the Swan. He was sitting at a table, his feet up on a stool, drinking from a mug of ale.

"Ah, young Master Shakespeare," Burbage said. "You've caught me taking a brief rest. But why the glum face, lad?"

Will hesitated. He didn't know where to start and so he gabbled everything to Burbage – his suspicions about Francis Peele, the threats Sir Thomas Lucy had made, what his parents had said as he listened at the door. Soon Burbage was sitting bolt upright, his eyes fixed on Will's, his face grim. At last Will finished his tale, but Burbage said nothing.

"I'm sorry, did I do right?" Will asked. "Maybe I've got it wrong ..."

"Don't worry, Will, you did *exactly* the right thing, and I thank you for it. You're very brave

to have spoken to me about this." Burbage
rubbed his beard in thought. "I hope you're
mistaken, but I've a nasty feeling you might not
be. We'd better have a word with our Mr Peele."

Burbage called for Cuthbert and asked him
to fetch Peele, and he soon came back with
the young player. Richard had tagged along,
curious to know what was going on. He sat
beside his father and looked at Will. Will said
nothing. Burbage told Cuthbert to shut the
door.

"Sit down, Peele," Burbage said. "I need to
ask you a question."

Peele looked at each of them in turn and his
Adam's apple bobbed up and down in his skinny
throat as he swallowed.

"Are you a spy sent from Spain?" Burbage
demanded.

Both Cuthbert and Richard looked at their father in alarm. Peele's face drained of any colour that was left in it.

"Of course not," Peele spluttered. He nodded at Will. "Has this rascal boy said something? He's nothing but a mischief-maker."

The room crackled with tension as Burbage stared hard at Peele. All of a sudden he grabbed him, lifting the younger man off his seat and ramming him up against the wall. He held him there, with his arm across Peele's throat, their faces almost touching. Will knocked over his own seat as he leaped to his feet.

"The only person making mischief here is you, Peele," Burbage said, his voice full of menace. "I'll ask you again. Are you a spy?"

Peele struggled, his eyes wild, but Burbage was too strong. "No," Peele said. "But I do have a mission and I will tell you what it is."

Chapter 8
In a Pickle

Burbage released his grip and Peele collapsed onto the floor, coughing and gasping.

"Help him back onto his seat, Cuthbert, and give him some ale," Burbage said.

Cuthbert did as he was told, and before long Peele was sitting stock still, staring at Burbage, his pale eyes full of hate and fear.

Will was a bit shaken by what he had seen. He had always known Burbage was tough. He was good-hearted and kind, but Will could see

it was a bad idea to get on the wrong side of him.

"Well?" Burbage demanded. "Let's hear it."

"I swear I'm no spy or assassin," Peele said. "I only want to bring people back to the true Church. I travel with you as a way of spreading the Word of God."

Will saw what a relief it was for Peele to let go of the strain of keeping his dangerous secret. He seemed younger now, more like a boy than a man. His family was Catholic, he explained, and he had spent time studying in Rome. Then he had decided to return to England.

"Is money what this is about? Are you after a reward?" Peele asked Burbage. "I do God's work while you sell your souls to the Devil ..."

"Spare us the sermon," Burbage said with a sigh. "I don't care if there is a reward. I don't care what religion you are – that's between you and your God. But I do care that you've put us all in danger. And you aren't even up to scratch as a player. Everything about you is so shifty and sly that people can't help but think you're a spy."

Peele shrunk a little into himself when he heard that. "I'm sorry I deceived you," he said. "Why don't I just leave? I swear to God I won't ever tell anyone I was one of your players."

"It might be too late for that," Burbage said. "The hounds of hell are already tracking you down. Tell him what you told me, Will. Cuthbert and Richard need to hear it as well."

So Will told them about Sir Thomas's hunt for a secret priest or a spy. Peele dropped his

51

head into his hands. Cuthbert and Richard looked as tough as their father.

"I have no fear of torture or death," Peele said at last. His voice was steady, but his hands shook.

"Then you're a damned fool," Burbage snorted. "And if they catch you, others will die too. We are all in a pickle, and no mistake."

"I say we let him go," Cuthbert said.

"No, he's too stupid to get away on his own," said Burbage. "Men like him *want* to die. He wants to be caught, and we can't let that happen."

"Who's going to catch him?" Richard said with a shrug. "No one here has a clue."

"I wouldn't be so sure," Burbage said. "This Sir Thomas may know what he's about. We

need a safe way of making Peele disappear and fast ..."

Will shook his head. He'd heard talk of helping people disappear ... who had it been? And then he remembered – his parents whispering by the fire. *"He's always known we helped Keating disappear ..."*

"I might know someone who could help," Will said.

The others turned to look at him. Will almost wilted under the heat of their gaze.

"Is that so, Will?" Burbage said.

Will nodded. "I just need to talk to –"

"*Stop*," Burbage said. He jumped to his feet, grabbed Will by the arm and led him towards the door. "Keep an eye on Peele, boys. We won't be long."

Outside, Burbage led him to a gloomy corner of the courtyard. "Don't say any more," he said.

Will opened his mouth, but Burbage held his hand up. "No, don't tell me," he said. "But are you sure you can help, Will?"

"Yes, I am," he said.

Burbage stared at him, his eyes fixed on Will's as if he was peering deep into his soul. He squeezed Will's arm. "Your word is good enough for me, Will Shakespeare," he said. "But whatever you do, be sure and do it soon."

Will nodded. Then he turned on his heel and hurtled home like the wind.

Will's mother was shelling peas into a bowl in the kitchen. He paused in the door to look at

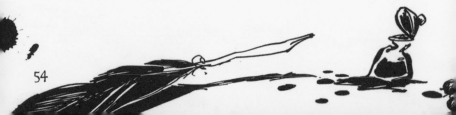

her and felt a surge of guilt. The last thing she needed was more trouble. But what else could he do?

"Ah, there you are," she said, throwing a peapod at Will. "I could do with some help ..."

"Mother, I know the man Sir Thomas is hunting," he said.

The peas scattered everywhere as Will's mother knocked the bowl over.

"Tell me," she said. "Tell me everything."

Chapter 9
A Sea of Troubles

"Francis Peele has gone," Will's mother told him the next morning. "None of the players has ever heard of him."

"But won't he get caught?" Will asked. "Or the people who helped him? Who was it, Mother?"

"All you need to know is that he'll have left England before the week is out," she said. "I'll be glad when the players leave town, too. Your father is right, Will. With friends like that you could end up drowning in a sea of troubles."

"But they didn't know that Peele was ..."

"Hush," she whispered, putting a finger to her lips. They were alone in the kitchen, but she still looked uneasy. "Let's just be glad that now Sir Thomas Lucy has no power over us."

Will smiled. He loved the idea that he had spoiled Sir Thomas's twisted schemes.

That evening the company put on the play Will had read with Richard – *The Terrible Tragedy of Hector, Prince of Troy*.

Cuthbert ruled the stage as the noble warrior Hector, Burbage played Hector's father brilliantly, and Richard made for a very beautiful Helen of Troy.

"Have you a minute, Will?" Burbage said as the courtyard cleared after the show. "I'd like a word with you."

Will nodded, and Burbage led him into the room where they had talked to Peele. He closed the door, and all of a sudden Will felt panicked. Had Peele's disappearance been too good to be true? Had something gone wrong?

"Don't look so worried, Will," Burbage said. "Everything is fine. I just want to thank you for what you did. I will be for ever in your debt."

"You're welcome," Will said, relieved. "I'm glad I could help."

"You did more than help, Will – you saved our lives. You've showed yourself to be brave and loyal, and cool in a crisis. You've mucked in with us, and I know you have the makings of a player. So, I'd like to make you an offer.

Will you join our company, young Master Shakespeare?"

Will's soul leaped with joy. "If it was up to me I'd say yes in a heartbeat," he said. "But my father ..."

"Ah well, I've been thinking about that, and I have a plan," Burbage said with a smile. "I worry all the time about my boys' future – and I'm sure your father is the same. So we have to convince him. We have to show him that it's a good living, a good life."

Burbage told Will how people in London just couldn't get enough of plays, so much so that he had been able to build a permanent home for his company in London. The Theatre was a round, vaulted building, open to the sky.

"There's space for thousands of people, and we perform every day except Sunday," Burbage

said. "Think about it, Will – a penny a head for those who stand, more for the rich who want to sit. That's a fortune, Will. I've even started paying writers to write plays for my company. A talented writer could do really well for himself."

Will drank it all in. 'What must it feel like,' he wondered, with a thrill of excitement, 'to create a brand new story, one that everyone loves?' Probably even better than being the player who spoke the words. In fact, Will realised in a flash, the play was the most important part. Without a great story and great words, the actors were nothing.

"I know you're right," he said, and his voice fell flat. "But I know what my father will say."

"He'll say we're not *respectable*," Burbage said. "But what if you tell him Queen Elizabeth herself has visited my wonderful Theatre?"

"Has she really?" Will asked.

Burbage winked. "Well, your father won't know one way or the other, will he?"

And so, Will hurried home, plotting how to talk his father round. The offer was simple. Burbage would take him to London, give him a room, train him in all a player needed to know, and pay him as he learned. That door into the future had swung wide open and Will could see a glorious life ahead. Could he make his father see it too?

Will's father was waiting for him at the foot of the stairs.

"So you've bothered to come home at last," he said, his voice menacing in the gloom. "You've got some explaining to do, my lad."

Will felt his heart sink into his shoes.

Chapter 10
Not Just Empty Words

"Well?" Will's father snapped. "What have you got to say for yourself? Don't dare deny it. You've been seeing the players. You've been missing school. And, what's more, your mother's been part of it. Fools and liars, the pair of you."

"I'm sorry, Father," Will said. "I didn't mean to disobey you, truly I didn't. It's just – I couldn't resist ..."

"Ridiculous! I've never heard such nonsense in my life!"

Will's mother interrupted. "Let him speak, John. Listen to the boy."

Will took a deep breath and began. He talked about losing himself in the story of a play, about being thrilled and scared, about the power of the plays to make him laugh or cry. And he talked about how he would love to be a player himself.

At last he fell silent. His father shook his head as heavily as an old bear. "Most fathers would beat you to within an inch of your life for what you've done, Will," he said. "But I forgive you. All the same, you can't be a player."

"Why not?" said Will. "Burbage says there's money and fame to be made. He's made me an offer. He'll take me on, train me and pay me. I'll live with his company in London –"

"London?" his mother said. "You can't go there, Will. You're only a boy."

Will took a deep breath and let it out. "You're wrong about the players," he said. "They're good and kind, they work hard and they make people happy. If you were to meet Burbage he'd set your minds at ease. I know you both want the best for me, but –"

"Will, stop," his father said. "I'm sorry, but the answer is no."

"What if I go anyway?" he asked.

"Then you will be no son of mine," his father said.

"And that will break my heart," said his mother.

Will felt hot tears stinging his eyes, and he didn't want to cry in front of his parents. So he fled upstairs to his room. He lay in

bed with wild thoughts tumbling in his head. How could he change his father's mind? Every time he came up with another argument, he remembered his mother and his soul felt sick with guilt.

In the end, Will knew he had only one choice.

In the morning, Will went off to school as meek and gentle as could be. Doctor Pinch glowered at him, but Will took no notice. When the bell rang at noon, he left school and headed for the Swan, where Burbage was sitting at his favourite table with a mug of ale and a plate of bread and cheese.

"Ah, Master Shakespeare," he said with his easy grin. "I take it you've come to tell me how the battle went with your father. Did you win?"

"Far from it," said Will, and Burbage's grin faded. "I'm sorry, Mr Burbage. I'd love to accept your offer, but I can't."

"And I'm sorry to hear it," said Burbage. "Are you sure? Is there nothing I can do? Would a word with your father help?"

"I don't think so. You won't change my father's mind, and my mother thinks London is a den of vice."

"Well, I'm sorry," Burbage said. "But my offer stays open, Will, and you must come and see me in London if your parents ever change their minds."

"They won't," said Will. "They're both as stubborn as bears."

"But bears can be led by the nose," Burbage said. "And life can be full of surprises, mark my words."

Chapter 11
A Final Performance

Three days later, on Saturday, the players put on their final performance at the Swan before they left Stratford.

Will was determined to go. His father would be angry, but Will no longer cared about his father's rage. No punishment could be worse than making him turn down Burbage's offer.

The play was *Robin Hood*. It was even better than before, but for Will, it was bittersweet. As the final whistles and whoops died down, he stayed in the courtyard to help pack up – and to say goodbye. The company were leaving that evening, heading for a village a dozen miles away.

"Take care of yourself, Will," Richard said as Cuthbert gave him a hand up into the back of a wagon. "I hope you don't get too bored here in the country."

"I'll survive," Will said with a smile. "And don't you get in too much trouble with your wicked London ways."

Richard laughed and waved as the wagon moved off. His father and Cuthbert waved as well, and a player struck up a merry tune on a flute. Will stood and watched the wagons cross the bridge over the River Avon, until he could see them no more.

For the next few days Will settled back into his old life and tried not to think about what Burbage and Richard and the rest of the company might be doing. No one seemed very happy at home. His mother was cross with Will and his brothers and sisters, and snappy with the servants. Will's father hid in his office most of the time.

Then one morning a letter came for Will's father. Moments later he emerged from his office and hurried out of the house with a satchel stuffed with papers under his arm. He only returned as the smaller children were getting ready for bed.

"Are you all right, John?" Will's mother asked.

Will felt little Anne grip his hand. The air seemed to crackle with dread.

"No, I am *not* all right," Will's father snapped, and he strode away to his chamber. He almost knocked over Will's mother as he pushed past her.

Shaken, Will's mother ordered the children to go to their rooms. But still Will could hear his father ranting and his mother talking in a soft and soothing voice. He crept out of his room and sat listening at the top of the stairs, but he couldn't make out what they were saying.

No one in the house had slept when early next morning five men hammered on the door and asked for John Shakespeare. Will knew right away that they were bad news. They were hard-faced and had the rough, burly look of farmers. John Shakespeare refused to see them.

The day after that, Will's father disappeared.

●

It wasn't unusual for John Shakespeare to be out all day and return home late. But by the evening of the next day, Will's mother was frantic. She was pacing round the kitchen, sighing and muttering prayers and making the Sign of the Cross. Finally, Will stood in her way.

"What's going on, Mother?" he said. "I can't bear to see you like this."

A single tear rolled down her cheek. "Oh, Will," she said. "I can't tell you, I *mustn't*. You're too young to deal with our troubles –"

"No I'm not," said Will. "I know it's about money. We're a family. I want to help, but how can I if you keep secrets from me?"

"You're right ..." his mother said. "Your father has such grand ideas about how we should live. But the glove business doesn't pay enough, and so he went into money-lending and trading in wool. But he doesn't have a licence. And now he must pay a heavy fine. It will ruin us ..."

It turned out that Will's father had other debts as well. He owed money to farmers for wool he wasn't allowed to sell. He'd borrowed money from bankers to lend out, and he'd borrowed from Uncle Edmund too. The deal was that Edmund would get Will's mother's farm if Will's father couldn't pay the money back – and of course he couldn't. And that's what Uncle Edmund had been planning for all along.

"Uncle Edmund should be ashamed," Will yelled. "And so should Father. How could he let things get so bad? Our whole life is built on a lie! The worst thing is that you stopped me becoming a player because it wasn't *respectable*! And Father's not respectable!"

More tears ran down his mother's cheeks. "Don't think badly of him, Will," she said. "He does his best for us. He wants the best for you. Oh, I wish he'd come home! I'm afraid he'll –"

She broke off, and Will felt his blood run cold. Did she think his father might kill himself? He looked into her eyes – and he saw that she did.

"Don't worry," he said, and he squeezed her hand. "I'll find him."

Will kissed the top of his mother's head. Then he turned and ran out into the night to seek his father.

Chapter 12

Another Son to Me

A full moon had risen, and the black and white houses of Stratford looked eerie under a wash of silver light. Will half expected to see ghosts drift out of the night-time shadows, but all he saw was a fat rat scuttling away from the sound of his running feet.

He came to the market square and stopped to get his breath back. His stomach was twisted into a knot with anger and fear. Where could his father be? Stratford wasn't a big town, but it was big enough. There were hundreds of places a man could go and not be

found. And what about the river? The Avon was deep, and the current was strong …

Sudden loud voices broke the dead hush of the night. Will looked round and saw two men coming out of the Boar's Head. They were talking in a pool of dim light that spilled onto the square from the inn's open door. The men staggered off, their arms round each other, and Will headed towards the inn. Maybe someone in there might know where his father had gone.

The inn was crowded and noisy. Will looked for familiar faces, but he didn't recognise anyone. He was about to leave when the crowd parted and he caught a glimpse of his father slumped in a booth on the far side of the inn. Will felt a wave of relief that his father was all right, but it soon crashed on the rocks of his anger.

There was a row of empty bottles on the table in front of John Shakespeare, and he was resting his head on his arms. Will grabbed him and shook him hard.

"Father, what are you doing!" he hissed. "Mother is worried sick."

John Shakespeare sat up and tried to focus on Will. He was blind drunk, and now Will felt disgusted as well as angry.

"Poor Mary," he said, and he started to sob. "She deserves better than me. I've let her down. I've let you all down. I'm so sorry."

Will felt his anger and disgust drain away. He wanted to hate his father, but it was impossible with his father's suffering so plain to see. Deep down, Will knew that his father was a good man. But he had made a rotten mess of things.

"You can't just give up, Father," he said. "There must be something we can do."

His father shook his head. "I've tried everything, Will. And, you know, all I need is a few pounds. Just a bit of a breathing space. But nobody will lend me another penny."

He laid his head down again in a burst of self-pity, and Will was afraid that he might fall asleep. It was time to get him moving. Will asked a couple of men to help, and they hauled him to his feet. The landlord and the other men laughed as Will man-handled his father out the door.

When they at last staggered home, Will helped his mother get his father into bed. He curled up like a baby, sobbing, "Sorry ... so sorry ... so sorry," until he fell asleep.

Will's own mind was racing too fast for sleep. He kept thinking about those "few pounds" his father needed. Will had no money of his own. But did he know someone who might help?

The next morning Will set off before daylight. The town was silent as he hurried along the deserted streets and over the bridge. A farmer in a cart stopped and offered him a ride. They rolled along the road as the sun burned away the blanket of mist that covered the fields. A couple of hours later the farmer stopped at a church and Will hopped down with a word of thanks.

Will found Burbage's three wagons lined up on the village green. Burbage was climbing out of one as Will approached.

"Well met, young Master Shakespeare!" he said with a surprised grin. But then his face took on a serious expression. "I hope you haven't come with bad news."

"Oh no," Will said. "This isn't about, er ... the problem we had before. I've come to ask a favour, Mr Burbage. My father has got into a spot of trouble."

Burbage smoothed down his beard as Will explained. "So how can I help?" he asked. "Are you in need of a loan?"

"Yes, Mr Burbage," Will said and he crossed his fingers. "Please."

"Done," Burbage said. "I'm glad to have a chance to help you, as you helped me. But you'll have to pay me back – by coming to work for me."

Burbage spat in his palm and held out his hand. "Deal?" he asked.

Will smiled and did the same. The two shook hands. "Deal," Will said.

Later that day Burbage rolled up in a cart to the Shakespeares' house in Henley Street. Will's father was hungover and grumpy. He didn't want to take a single coin from Burbage.

"Don't be so stupid, John," said Will's mother. "Take the money and let Will go. Mr Burbage will look after him."

"You can depend on that," Burbage said. "He'll be another son to me."

Will's father stared at him. Then he nodded, and that was that.

Two days later Will was on his way to London.

Chapter 13
Good Night Unto You All

London, 1599

"Begging your leave, Mr Shakespeare," the boy in the doorway said. "Your guests have arrived."

Will put down his quill and tidied the papers on his desk. The new play was taking shape, and he knew in his heart that it was good. He would call it *Hamlet*.

"Hand me that scroll, will you, Ned?" he said. Ned passed the scroll to Will with a little bow. Will tucked it under his arm, and then he went down to the yard.

They had only finished the new building a month ago, and the company was still settling in. It was bustling with life and energy, and Will knew they would do good work here. They'd called it The Globe. It seemed right for this round theatre, open to the London sky, where they would tell stories of faraway times and places.

Will's only regret was that Burbage never saw The Globe. His old friend had died two years ago. Will was sure he would have approved of the building, created from the wood of Burbage's old Theatre north of the River Thames. Will, Richard and Cuthbert were all rich men now, and The Globe promised to be the most successful of all London's theatres.

"Looks like a fine crowd, Mr Shakespeare," Ned said.

The gates were open and people were flooding in. Some pointed at Will, but he was used to being famous and took delight in it now. It had been a long time since he had been a boy like Ned, fetching and carrying, cleaning and mending, taking the money and running errands for the company. All the while learning to act, and beginning to write.

Writing was practically all Will did these days. It suited him well. There was nothing like the feeling of finishing a play and knowing the crowd would love it.

Will's guests turned as he approached.

"Welcome, Mother and Father," he said. "I trust you had a good journey?"

His mother said, "Yes," just as his father said, "No."

They were older now, and they had seen great sadness. Gilbert and Richard and Joan were all living their grown-up lives. But little Anne had died from the plague the year after Will had left for London. Will understood their pain – his own son Hamnet had been taken by the plague when he was only eleven and Will's sadness had been deeper than any ocean.

To change the subject, he said, "Look, Father, I have something for you."

Will handed his father the scroll and his father's eyes grew wide as he unrolled the parchment and saw the striking yellow and black image upon it. A Coat of Arms for the Shakespeare family, complete with a motto in French. *"Non sans droit"* – "Not without right."